A Green
PENGUIN

To Rex

I hope you enjoy

Blaqbu

A Green PENGUIN

by

Brian Cooper

BROWN DOG BOOKS

Published under licence by Brown Dog Books and
The Self-Publishing Partnership, 7 Green Park Station,
Bath BA1 1JB

www.selfpublishingpartnership.co.uk

ISBN printed book: 978-1-78545-371-7

Cover design by Andrew Prescott
Internal design by Andrew Easton

Printed and bound in the UK

Chapter 1

A Nice Surprise

It was the school holidays and Hayden was looking forward to all sorts of exciting things to do. When you are eight years old it's difficult to run around all day. It's OK if your friend Josh comes over to stay – you can play all sorts of games – but Hayden didn't always want to be hot and bothered. Sometimes he liked it nice and quiet. Really, Hayden didn't know what he wanted to do! Summer, summer, summer. He always had his PlayStation and the games on it, including Minecraft and Batman, but sometimes it was good to experience new things, new adventures, new friends. How was he going to do that?

In the garden, his little sister Izzy was busy getting out of breath on the big trampoline Dad had put up in the garden. It was good, but bouncing up and down did get boring after a while! Hayden wanted something different. Something that would be fun but also a challenge. Not much chance of that where he lived. It looked as if it was going to be a long, boring summer holiday.

He could annoy his sister, after all she always annoyed him! No, he thought. That would only cause an argument with his mum and he didn't want to spend the holiday in solitary confinement shut away in his room without his games. He resigned himself to the fact that he would just have to wait and see what fate had in store for him. It turned out that he didn't have to wait very long.

A week after the end of term, Hayden's mum and dad had a surprise for him and Izzy. After they had all finished their tea and Hayden and his sister were cleaning their teeth ready for bed, Mum told them that they had booked a holiday at the seaside. Izzy was so excited that she nearly swallowed her toothbrush. "When, when, when? Where are we going? Are we going on a plane? Are we going on a train? Are we going on the bus?"

Their mum laughed. "Whoa, slow down, all in good time. Now, finish your teeth and get into bed."

That night, neither Hayden nor Izzy got much sleep. They were far too excited about the holiday.

They chatted and giggled about where they could be going. Hayden said they wouldn't be going on a plane because they didn't have passports.

"What's a passport?" asked Izzy.

He explained that it was a piece of paper you needed to visit another country.

"Oh!" said Izzy none the wiser. It was all a mystery until tiredness overtook and they finally fell asleep.

Packing for holidays was always a hassle. Mum was beginning to shout and Dad was trying to do his best and making things worse. Don't forget this and don't forget that. You don't need this, you don't need that, and of course everybody always packs too much.

"Get out of my way and I'll do the packing for everyone!" cried Mum.

It was utter confusion. Chaos was the order of the day. Finally, everything was ready for the big day and peace and quiet settled around the house.

"Can you tell us where we are going?" asked Hayden. "Or is it a secret?"

Mum was busy with the cases so it was Dad who told them. "We are going to Tumbledown Cove. A small village by the seaside."

Izzy let out a scream, "Yeah, the seaside! Yippee." Hayden was less noisy but just as pleased. He did like the seaside but not those busy places with all the music, noise and rides. He liked to be quiet. Tumbledown Cove sounded perfect.

Chapter 2

Tumbledown Cove

Tumbledown Cove was a delightful little village on a coastal clifftop overlooking a large bay and smaller coves. It had a small harbour with only two fishing boats tied to the jetty, and the fishermen were cleaning the decks. The seagulls kept a careful watch, circling overhead for any scraps of fish. It all looked like a picture postcard.

After settling into their cottage, the whole family agreed they should go off and explore. They first went into the village. It was very quiet. No cars speeding by, no loud radios only a friendly "Hello" from the few people they saw on the only street. The village shop looked as if it had come out of the history books. It sold everything from fruit and veg to headache pills and DVDs. It was also the village post office, and who could fail to notice jar upon jar of sweets of every kind lined up on the shelves. Boiled sweets, toffee sweets, humbugs and jelly fruits. Izzy's eyes sparkled at the sight. Hayden looked around. Why couldn't everywhere be like this instead of being noisy and smelly, dirty and full of traffic with people rushing and shoving, caring only for what they had to do? He was deep in thought. Was it ever like Tumbledown everywhere once upon a time? What changed? Was it the people?

The steps down to the beach were not easy to

use, twisting and undulating down the cliff face. Thankfully, there was a safety rail that they could hold on to as they went up and down. The side of the cliff was covered in small flowers, and there were curious holes everywhere. Hayden was intrigued and was going to find out more about those holes!

By the time they had all reached the bottom, had a quick look round and climbed back up the steps, they were all very warm. The sun was still shining even though it was now teatime. They stopped at the village shop and all had an ice cream, Yes, the shop even sold ice creams and lollies! Hayden devoured his quicker than you could blink. Wow, that was cold but delicious, he thought. Just the thing when you're hot.

"Wake up, sleepyhead!" Hayden opened his

eyes with a start! "Your breakfast is on the table," Hayden could hear his mum calling. Whatever was the time? Everybody was up and dressed and he was still in bed! Hayden quickly washed and cleaned his teeth, put on his clothes and headed for the kitchen.

"Good morning," said his mum. "Did you have a good sleep? It was long enough. We are all off to the beach today and I am making some sandwiches for us to have for lunch. Mum gave them both a smile, "What would you two like in yours?"

Hayden and Izzy both spoke at the same time, "Sardines and cucumber please!"

Their mum looked at them both in disbelief. "Ok, whatever next?"

It was a lovely sunny day with just a gentle

breeze as they made their way down the steps to the beach. Again, Hayden saw those holes in the cliff, but this time he also saw birds flying in and out them! Strange, he thought. Don't birds live in nests in trees? Something to research when he got home. That night he found out that the birds he saw were called 'Sand Martins' and that they make their homes in the cliff face away from danger.

The big beach stretched a long way and there was plenty of space to play. Other children on the beach were playing ball games and digging sandcastles. Once they were settled, Izzy started to dig and asked Hayden to help but he wanted to explore. He asked his dad if he could go over to the rocks and his dad said yes, but he must come back as soon as they called.

"OK I will," said Hayden. Grabbing his swimming goggles and spade he set off.

Chapter 3

The Secret Cove

Hayden had his rubber beach shoes on but even so some the rocks were sharp and he had to be careful not slip or he would cut himself. There were plenty of little pools in the rocks and he could see some starfish and crabs but he hadn't brought a bucket.

Once he was over the rocks he found himself in a very quiet secluded cove with a sandy beach. Wow, thought Hayden. This could be my special place, it's perfect. Then he took another look and in the far corner of the cove he observed what looked like a big heap of rubbish. Strange, he thought. What's a big pile of rubbish doing in such a nice place? He went over for a closer inspection. The pile was made up of old fishing nets, plastic bags, children's old buckets, food containers and old newspaper. A lot of things that people had thrown away because they were no longer needed. None of this belongs on the beach, he thought. Well, it was rubbish, so Hayden took no further interest in the pile and moved off to the sea's edge.

The water looked warm. The waves were very small and lapped invitingly over his toes. Hayden wasn't the best of swimmers but he did like the water and enjoyed lots of diving under with his goggles on to protect his eyes so that he could see. He had done it lots of times in the swimming pool but this would be his first experience of diving in the sea. He was a little apprehensive. He was also excited about seeing what was there!

He put his right foot into the lapping water and felt it squeeze through his shoe and round his toes. It tickled! It didn't feel too cold and so he ventured further and now both feet were wet. Soon he was up to his knees and now the water was a little cooler. Thankfully, the waves were no bigger so he didn't have to jump to avoid them. He plucked up his courage and suddenly he dropped, and both his shoulders were underwater. This time he did jump! Yikes! he thought. That was a bit of a shock. The coldness of the water took his breath away but he quickly recovered and somehow felt warmer. "Oh, that's OK," he thought to himself and ducked under again, this time with no surprises.

Time to see what's lurking under the water, he thought. He reminded himself of his visit to the sea life centre and all the fish he saw. I wonder if I will see anything? he thought. Certainly not a great white shark, that would be silly! Was he trying to convince himself that it would be ok? Was he just a little bit unsure of what he would see? "Don't be stupid," he told himself. "It'll be fine." This was not the swimming pool but the sea. "It's now or never," he said, and he set his goggles over his eyes and prepared to see under the sea for the very first time.

Chapter 4

An Underwater Encounter

At first it was very difficult for Hayden to see anything because of all the sand he had kicked up when he went into the water, but slowly it began to clear. He could see the bottom and his own feet. Gasping, he brought his head out of the water. "Must remember I can't breathe under water," he said to himself. He took a deep breath. With lungs full of air, he put his head back under.

The water had cleared even more and he could make out stones and a tiny crab on the bottom. This is better than building sandcastles, he thought. He came up for more air and then bobbed down again. Suddenly in front of him he thought he saw a penguin! "Now you are being silly. A penguin – don't be daft!"

He took a fresh breath and looked again. Nothing. He must have imagined it. Cautiously he looked again. This time it was so close it had to be real! Hayden stood up in the water, so did the penguin. Not sure what to do, Hayden backed out of the water onto the beach, closely followed by the penguin.

"Hello," said the penguin. Hayden fell over. A talking penguin, on a beach, on his holiday? He must be dreaming. "Hello," said the penguin again.

Sitting on the beach, Hayden looked at the

penguin in disbelief. "Hello," he said back.

The penguin came closer. "My name's Dylan," he said. "What's yours?"

Hayden introduced himself.

"Hayden," said Dylan. "What does that mean? My name means 'son of the sea'."

"Oh," said Hayden. "I don't know what mine means."

Chapter 5

Dylan's Story

"I'm a humboldt penguin," said Dylan.

"Yes, I know," said Hayden. "I love penguins, they're my favourite.

"Your favourite what?" asked Dylan.

"Just my favourite," said Hayden. "I like reading about them and I have some model penguins in my bedroom at home. I know that humboldt penguins live in Peru in South American, which is a long way away so what are you doing here?"

"That," said Dylan, "is a sad story."

My parents were captured and brought to England on a boat and put in the sea life centre just up the coast from here so that people could see them. They were treated well but they missed their home and friends. I was born in the sea life centre. My mum and dad told me all about their lives and how they got here and that they should really be free and swimming and living in the sea. I made my mind up that, given the chance, I would try to escape and live the life they talked about. Sadly, both my parents died and I was left alone. Being fed twice a day and swimming in circles wasn't much fun and the other penguins weren't interested in making friends so I hatched my plot to escape. I had nothing to stay for at the sea life centre. My life was going nowhere.

The centre also looked after stray or injured

seals. They would feed them and the doctor would look at them and try to make them better. When they were strong enough, the seals would be taken to the beach and released into the sea. I saw this as my opportunity and began to hatch my plan of escape.

The seals were kept in a compound close by and I could watch as the keepers went to and fro, and I saw how they moved the seals ready for their release.

On the next release day, I was ready, and when the opportunity came, I jumped into the seal enclosure and quickly got into the water bag that they carried the seals in. Luckily for me I wasn't seen and they put a young seal in my bag. I could feel the movement as we were put onto the lorry. It was only a short journey and soon we were at the beach. My bag was carried into the water and opened. As soon as the seal made its move I followed. We made a big splash! I heard one of the keepers say, "Wow, that little one's in a hurry." I had made it. I quickly swam away from the beach into the open sea. I lay on my back and looked back at the beach and I could see the keepers leaving. I breathed a big sigh of relief. Free.

Later, I met up with the seal again and we became friends. I called him Slim because he was slim, unlike other seals who can be rather large, if you know what I mean? I told him my name was Dylan but he insisted on calling me Pengy the porpoise! How can you call me that? I asked him. He said it was because I kept jumping out of the water like a porpoise!"

Looking at Hayden Dylan said that penguins

couldn't breathe under the water and so had to come up for air, the same as he did, but because they swim so quickly, when they come up they leave the water like a rocket, take a deep breath and then dive back down. "Did you know," said Dylan, "even your animal scientists call that porpoising! So, I guess Slim was right in a way, haha!"

"Hayden!" It was Dad calling.

"I've got to go now," Hayden said. "I can't believe what's happened today. Will you be here tomorrow?"

"Of course," said Dylan. "See you then and we can talk and swim some more."

"Come on," said his mum. "Your sardine and cucumber sandwiches are going cold!"

Hayden laughed. He loved his mum. "Mum,

do you know what my name Hayden means?"

"No," said his mum. "What made you think of such a thing?

"Well," Hayden paused, "I was wondering why this place is called Tumbledown Cove. I guess something must have happened like a rockfall and then it set me thinking about what we call other things and why. My name seemed a good place to start, that's all."

"My my," His mum gave him a funny look. "What a strange thing to think about. Well, we called you Hayden because we like the name. We didn't think about what it meant. Anyway, what have you been up to?" she asked. "You've been gone a while and we were getting a bit worried."

"Sorry," said Hayden." I was just mucking about on the beach with my goggles to see if there were any fish, but I didn't see any."

"Never mind," said his dad. "Maybe tomorrow."

Yes, thought Hayden. Maybe tomorrow!

Chapter 6

A Scary Story

Hayden was up bright and early the next morning. No lie-in today, he thought. It was another lovely sunny day and everybody was soon ready for the beach. Izzy wanted Hayden to play with her because it was no fun on her own. Hayden really wanted to go to his cove but also knew that if he made too much fuss then Mum and Dad would want to know more, and so he agreed. After a while, Hayden actually started to enjoy himself, and the morning sped by.

After lunch, Hayden ran off towards the cove. He didn't have to wait long before Dylan arrived. "Hello," said Dylan. "I was watching you arrive at the beach with your mum, dad and sister. You're very lucky. You have a lovely family. I really miss my mum and dad."

Hayden felt a bit guilty that he didn't play with his sister more often.

"Have you seen that pile of rubbish in the corner of the cove?" Hayden asked Dylan.

"Of course I have," he said. "I put it there!"

"What?" said Hayden. "Why?"

"Time for another story," said Dylan.

"One day, Slim and I were swimming and playing in the water just out from the cove when suddenly I felt as if I was being strangled and dragged to the sea bottom. I was very scared and started to panic because I didn't have any air in my lungs. I twisted and turned as violently as I could and somehow managed to get to the surface and grab some air. My throat was still tight and it was difficult to swim. It was like a heavy weight round my neck. I struggled ashore and collapsed, gasping for breath. Again, I shook my head and this time I managed to free myself from whatever had a hold on me. After a short while I recovered enough to see what it was.

It was a plastic bag from the local shop. Somehow, while I was swimming, I had managed to get my head through the handle of the bag and of course the bag filled with water and acted like an anchor dragging me down. As I stood on the beach getting my breath back it gave me time to think about what might have happened.

Just then, a seagull flew down next to me squawking loudly. I turned to see what he was making all the fuss about and I couldn't believe what I saw. He too was caught up in plastic. His head was through one loop and his foot was through another. It was the kind of plastic used to keep cola cans together. I quickly bit through the loops and helped him to get free, and with a thanks he flew off.

It made me think and wonder. What was going on? I quickly realised that there must be a lot of this rubbish floating around the sea or lying on the beaches, and more birds or fish could get hurt. So, I decided to start my own clean-up campaign."

Chapter 7

Many Hands Make Light Work

"It sounds like you and the seagull were very lucky. It must have been very scary. I can understand why you want to clear the rubbish. I think it's a great idea," said Hayden. "There are some silly people about leaving their rubbish everywhere. They don't know the dangers they cause to others."

"I do this every day, if I can," said Dylan.

"Can I help you today?" said Hayden.

"Many hands make light work," said Dylan. "That means we can get it done quicker."

Together they set to work. Throughout the afternoon, Hayden and Dylan worked tirelessly collecting all the rubbish they could see. Dylan would swim out to sea and drag back bits of netting and pieces of wood while Hayden would pick them from the shoreline and carry them to the pile.

Suddenly, Dylan disappeared! Hayden look around. Coming over the rocks was his dad.

"What have you been doing, Hayden?" his dad asked and then he paused when he saw the pile of rubbish. "Have you been doing this? Is this rubbish that you have collected?"

Hayden couldn't tell his dad about Dylan. He would never believe him. "Yes it is. Isn't it a shame that people leave so much rubbish on the beach? Why don't they take it home with them?"

His dad agreed with him and told Hayden he was proud of him for being so thoughtful and hard-working clearing the beach. "Now I know what you've been up to, I'll go back and tell your mum and you can carry on until we call you. Well done, I'm proud of you."

After his dad had climbed back over the rocks, Dylan reappeared. "Your dad's alright," said Dylan. "I like him."

Hayden laughed. "Where does all the rubbish go once you have piled it all up?" asked Hayden.

"Well," said Dylan, "the people in the town think that one of them is collecting all this stuff and so once a week a big lorry comes along and the men put it all onboard and they drive off! I don't know where they go but they leave the beach ready for the next pile. Sometimes there's a lot and sometimes not. In the summer, it is mostly stuff that people leave behind on the beach like food wrappers or old newspapers and empty drink cans. In the winter, it's stuff washed up on the beach by the storms, mostly things from passing ships."

Hayden was looking down at the sand, "I'm afraid I have some sad news Dylan. This is my last day with you. My holiday comes to an end tomorrow and I have to go home. I am really going to miss you and helping you. You are doing a great job and I wish I could stay longer. I will certainly remember this holiday and what you have shown me. I will be back next year and I promise that I will learn to swim so that I can go out with you and maybe meet up with Slim!"

"That would be great!" said Dylan. "You'll like

Slim. He can be a slippery customer in the water."

"I have had a super time with you and I will remember about all the rubbish we collected. I will make the effort to put all mine in the waste bin and not on the floor."

"Good for you," said Dylan.

"I really must go now or I'll get in trouble. Take care of yourself and don't go swimming near any shopping bags!"

Dylan laughed. "I won't," he said. "Have a safe journey home yourself."

They gave each other a hug and before Dylan could see the tears in Hayden's eyes, Hayden jumped up onto the rocks and was gone.

Chapter 8

Going Green

It was the start of a new term at school and Hayden was looking forward to it with some caution. He was going to be with new children and a new teacher, Mr. Daniels. Mr. Daniels was always smiling and friendly and softly spoken.

"Good morning everybody," said Mr. Daniels. "I hope you all had a lovely summer break. This term we will all be going green!" The class started to giggle aloud. "I don't mean like little spacemen," he said, "I mean we will be looking at how we live and how we look after where we live. The plants, the birds, animals and fish and the land. People use the word 'green' because it relates to the earth, probably because of the grass and the leaves on the trees. Scientists use the word 'eco', which comes from the word 'ecology'. That means the study of living things and where they live. People who do a lot of work trying to keep our planet healthy are called 'eco warriors' – great name, hey? If we don't look after the earth, it could die. Not today or tomorrow but a long time in the future, and that would be it. No more people, birds or animals!"

The class went very quiet.

"Not a nice thought, is it?" asked Mr. Daniels.

"OK," said Mr. Daniels. "Your first task this term is to write about your holiday and what you did.

Try to think what I just said and include things you might have done to help the planet. I know it's a big ask, but things like being tidy, not picking wild flowers all help. So, you can write a bit and add some pictures if you want to and later we will have a look at some of them."

Hayden knew exactly what he was going to write about, but how could he do it and not mention Dylan? After all, Dylan was the one responsible for the clean-up, not him. He realised that he would have to say it was him and hope that nobody found out.

It was hard work but Hayden enjoyed it, because the class was quiet and he could concentrate on his own story. He told it exactly as it happened, leaving out the bits involving Dylan, but he did put in the story that Dylan had told him about getting caught in the shopping bag. Finally, he drew a picture of the cove and the pile of rubbish.

Mr. Daniels called time and collected all the stories. "It's time for home now," he said. "I will take your stories home and read them. I will pick out some to read in class tomorrow. Well done, everyone. See you in the morning."

Hayden went home exhausted. Crikey, he thought. That was tough!

Chapter 9

A Green Penguin

The next morning, the children were all talking to one another about their stories. Hayden was ok with this because he got to know some of the new children, and having new friends is always a good thing.

"OK class, settle down." Mr. Daniels walked into the room. "I hope you all had a good night's sleep ready for more work today," he said. "Firstly, though, let's look at the work you all did yesterday about being green!"

Mr. Daniels read out several good stories from children who had cleaned their bedroom, helped their mum tidy the garden and one who had put up a bird table and built a bug hotel!

"Now," said Mr. Daniels, "I have a star story. One that shows what I mean about caring for the planet and helping save its future. Hayden, will you join me at the front of the class, please?"

Oh no, thought Hayden. He didn't like being the centre of attention. This was not good but yet it was, because of his story.

Mr. Daniels read out Hayden's story of his clean-up at Tumbledown Cove. He asked Hayden what made him do it in the first place. Hayden said that he had found a lovely cove but that it was full of rubbish that lazy people had left behind which was spoiling the beach. There was even broken glass that could cut your feet.

"I thought that if the rubbish could hurt me than it could also hurt the birds, and if it got into the sea it could hurt the fish as well, and so I decided to clear it all up."

Mr. Daniels presented Hayden with a star certificate saying that he was proud of him and that he should keep up the good work. His story was just what being an eco warrior was all about.

Hayden smiled. Wow, a warrior! That night, Hayden showed his mum and dad and Izzy the certificate that Mr. Daniels had given him. It read, 'Presented to Hayden for an excellent story. He is our first eco warrior.'

In his room, Hayden lay in bed thinking of Dylan, and hoped that he was proud too. There was no doubting that Dylan was not only an eco warrior, but he was also the one and only Green Penguin.

The end